MOUSE'S FIRST
Valentine

Lauren Thompson

ILLUSTRATED BY
Buket Erdogan

SIMON & SCHUSTER BOOKS FOR YOUNG READERS
New York ❤ London ❤ Toronto ❤ Sydney ❤ Singapore

To Robert and Owen ✑ L.T.

To my brother, Ibo; *dostum* Emel; and my dear
friends, Glenda and M.B. ✑ B.E.

SIMON & SCHUSTER BOOKS FOR YOUNG READERS
An imprint of Simon & Schuster Children's Publishing Division
1230 Avenue of the Americas, New York, New York 10020

Text copyright © 2002 by Lauren Thompson
Illustrations copyright © 2002 by Buket Erdogan
All rights reserved, including the right of reproduction in whole or in part in any form.
SIMON & SCHUSTER BOOKS FOR YOUNG READERS is a trademark of Simon & Schuster.

Book design by Paula Winicur
Printed in the United States of America
10 9 8 7 6 5 4 3 2 1
Library of Congress Card Number: 2001020600
ISBN 0-689-84724-6

Early one morning,
big sister Minka
sneaked into the house...

and so did little Mouse!

First, Minka creeped high and low
and all around
till she found something
smooth and rosy.

What could it be? wondered Mouse.

"Red paper!" said Minka.
"Just what I need."

Next, Minka raced over and and all around under till she found something white and holey.

What could it be? wondered Mouse.

"Lace!" said Minka.
"Just what I need."

Now Minka leaped here... there and all around till she found something shiny and curly.

What could it be? wondered Mouse.

"Ribbon!" said Minka.
"Just what I need."

Then Minka peeked inside
and outside
and all around
till she found something
sticky and goopy.

What could it be? wondered Mouse.

"Paste!" said Minka.
"Just what I need."

Then Mouse watched Minka
fold the paper here.

**and brush
the paste there . . .**

and smooth
the lace here...

and tie the ribbon there.

"It's ready!" said Minka.

What is it? wondered Mouse.

"Little Mouse!" called Minka.
"This valentine
is just for YOU
on Valentine's Day...